A Penny
for a Hundred

by Ethel Pochocki

pictures by Mary Beth Owens

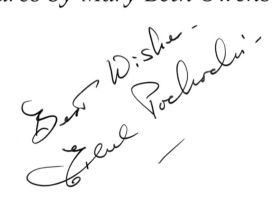

Best Wishes –
Ethel Pochocki

Down East Books / Camden, Maine

Dedicated to
the generous and hospitable people
of The County, who shared
their memories with me.

Early one morning in mid-July 1944, Clare woke and ran to the window, and there they were. She had been waiting for weeks for the potato field to blossom. Now, at last, she could see a handful of white flowers dotting the green vines. By end of day, they would be covered with the blossoms. Her father said they would be out by the fifteenth, just as the peas were ready by the fourth, and he was right. Her father was so smart.

From this day until October, their life would revolve around potatoes. Now mounding and hoeing and fertilizing, and then, the harvesting. The thought of it made Clare wiggle with excitement. It would be the first year she was old enough to pick with the other workers. Everyone in Aroostook County in northern Maine either owned a potato farm or picked potatoes. It was their livelihood. School let out for three weeks in the fall so children could help with the harvest, and this year she too would be with them, working outdoors and earning money. She could hardly wait!

She dressed quickly and made her bed even more quickly but not perfectly. Her mother was a stickler for tight sheets, but Clare knew she'd excuse a few lumps here and there today. She could smell the bacon being fried up and the coffee perking in the blue enamel pot and the sweet sauce cooking from the first raspberries. The honeysuckle winding its way around the porch railing gave off its morning fragrance, and Clare thought there was nothing so heavenly as the smells of a summer morning and the soft sound of her mother and father laughing in the kitchen, and the day all fresh and waiting for her!

This morning her mother, whose grandparents had come from Sweden, had made *Ugnspannkaka,* a Swedish pancake. She baked it in the cast-iron frying pan and it came out of the oven high and golden, puffed like a mushroom. Her mother cut it into three pieces and poured the raspberry sauce over it. She always made Swedish pancake on the day of first blossoms.

The talk at breakfast was of another exciting happening. Today the Germans were coming, her father said. Their first crew would be here this morning. Her parents looked serious and a little uneasy. Clare was more curious than frightened. She wanted to see what a German looked like. In the movies and cartoons and posters, they seemed to be ugly, angry monsters. She knew the Germans were the enemy of their country, and that her brother, Patrick, and her uncles and the mailman and the grocery boy at Bouchard's Market had gone overseas to fight them and make sure they didn't come over here.

And now they *were* coming over here, right here in Maine.

Her father explained to her that they were prisoners of war, German soldiers who had been captured, and rather than just put them in jail, they were being put to use to work in this country on cotton farms and in canneries and logging camps and potato fields. Her parents, like most of the townspeople, did not welcome them, for they were the enemy. Many of their friends' sons had died. And yet they were grateful for the help. There were few workers to replace the able-bodied men who had gone to war, and while Clare's mother and aunts did what they could, they also had to work their victory gardens, can vegetables, make preserves, take care of the laundry and animals. They could not be in two places at once. So without the prisoners' help, their crop and their neighbors' would freeze in the ground.

"We must be fair and treat them like human beings," said her father. "Wait and see how they act. They are probably wondering what we are like too."

Clare was eager to begin work in the field. Today and for many days after, she would pick potato bugs off the vines and drop them into a mayonnaise jar, keeping count as she worked. Her father paid her a penny for a hundred. She didn't like potato bugs. They were squishy and crawly in her fingers. The youngest children were always given this job, this and pulling mustard weed by hand, because they were the only ones who had the patience and eagerness to do it. And the pennies added up.

Clare was intent on catching the bugs unaware before they could scatter—she already had seventy-six in the jar—when she heard the truck coming down the dirt road into the field. She saw the twelve men in their baggy uniforms with PW stamped on the back of them, many of them young and smiling, some older and serious-looking. None looked unhappy to be there. One young prisoner with curly blond hair smiled at her. She looked down and didn't smile back. She thought, as she resumed catching the doomed bugs, that they didn't look much different from Patrick and her cousins.

Clare's father spoke briskly to them, explaining what he expected of them. The men took off their caps respectfully but seemed puzzled. The blond young man explained that none of the others spoke English—his father was a teacher and so he had learned English and French. "I was a soldier for one day and then captured," he smiled and shrugged. "Now I am in a potato field across the ocean. I much prefer this."

Among the other men, he said, there was a plumber, a lawyer, a clockmaker, a barber, and a minister. "No farmers," he said, "but we shall learn." Clare's father laughed and walked away.

The men went to work mounding up the potato hills so the new potatoes wouldn't get burnt by the sun. They talked softly among themselves in German as they did their job quickly and neatly. A guard sat nearby, watching them to make sure none tried to escape.

Clare's mother brought out some jugs of lemonade and fresh hot doughnuts. The men nodded their thanks, and Clare's mother nodded back politely. Perhaps, she thought, some German mother might treat her Patrick with similar kindness.

During the day, Clare found herself working in the row next to the young blond prisoner. She looked over once and caught him doing the same thing.

"Hello," he smiled, "what are you doing?"

"Picking potato bugs," she answered without looking up.

"Ugh," he shivered and made a face. "Why? Are you going to make a stew?"

She had to laugh at such a thought. "No, that would be pretty awful. I have to pick them off or else they'll kill the plants and then we'd have no potatoes. I get a penny for a hundred, and I'm going to get a nickel today," she said with pride.

"So much work. And you are so determined. I'm sure you will get your nickel," he smiled again and went back to hoeing.

A few minutes later, Clare asked, "What's your name?"

"Peter. What's yours?"

"Clare."

"Is that right? What do you know! I have a sister, Clara. She's a little older than you. She is away at music school in Austria. Or she was when I last heard."

"And I have an older brother, Patrick. He's in Belgium now."

That evening, before the prisoners returned to their camp, Peter came up to Clare and gave her a tobacco can filled with 304 potato bugs. He had picked them during his lunch break.

When Clare told her parents about this, they looked at each other. "That was very kind of him," said her mother. "Indeed it was," said her father.

During the days that followed, Clare and Peter became friends and told each other stories about their families and the towns they lived in, and it was almost as if he had always been there and they had always been friends. The lovely days of summer flew by quickly, then, one hot August afternoon, Clare heard the sound that usually made her sad, the first song of the cricket. This meant the end of summer, the start of school, and then the long siege of winter before she could run barefoot again. But this time, she didn't mind at all. She even wished autumn would hurry up, for this year she would be picking potatoes.

She had been to the field before, but she was a child then, sitting beneath the tree, watching the lunches while her mother picked. Now she was nine, and she could work and earn money like the others. Her friends and cousins bought new clothes and shoes with what they earned, or a new stove for the family, or saved the money for college.

There was nothing Clare especially wanted to buy. For sure she would take her parents to Thorborg's Ice Cream Parlor and they would each have a black-and-white soda or even a banana split with three scoops of ice cream. With Peter's help, she had already saved enough potato-bug money for this.

When the first day of picking finally arrived, Clare got up at 4:00 A.M., shivering in the dark as her feet touched the cold floorboards. She could see her breath in the frosty September air. She dressed in several layers of clothes and double socks. With quiet excitement, she ate her oatmeal and a thick slice of cornbread and blackberry jam, grabbed her lunch bucket, and rode off in the truck with her parents just as the night was fading from the sky.

The Germans were already there, huddled together and rubbing their hands.

"Where are your gloves?" asked Clare's father.

"We have none, sir," said Peter.

"You can't work without gloves," said Clare's father with impatience; "your fingers will freeze. The ground doesn't thaw until ten o'clock at best." He got into the truck and drove off towards town.

The horse-drawn one-row digger began its work churning the earth, rolling potatoes out of the ground like a ship cutting through water, exposing rows and rows of the newborn treasure for eager, sleepy workers to pick. It was like finding the eggs on Easter morning, Clare thought. Then a flatbed truck came between the rows, dropping off large wooden barrels every few yards to be filled.

Before the field was finished, Clare's father returned with twelve pairs of heavy work gloves. He handed them out to the prisoners saying gruffly, "Just want you to know we're human beings on this side of the ocean too. Now let's get to work!" And so they did.

What a scene it was that day and for the next few weeks, as children and neighbors and prisoners worked together under that expanse of brilliant blue sky that is part of northern Maine! Long lines of bending bodies, scooping potatoes into their woven ash baskets as fast as they could, others kneeling and shuffling along that way, fanning their hands out into large circles so none of the bounty could escape them.

Layers of clothes were taken off and then put back on, as sun and wind took turns making them melt and shiver, and as they worked, they teased and gossiped and told jokes, and the air was filled with the babble of French and English and Swedish and German and the one common language of laughter.

After lunch, Clare and her friends would play in the hayloft, and when they were bored of that, they got into mischief. They would hide in empty barrels or have potato fights. Once a badly aimed potato hit the diggerman and knocked his glasses off, and he growled at them to stop that horsing around right then and there. "You kids are like maggots on a dead horse!" he barked. But he chuckled to himself, remembering that he wasn't much different when *he* was picking.

Soon the harvest was done. The last potatoes had been picked and hauled off to the potato houses where they were stored until they were ready to be shipped out-of-state. The vines were burned, the fields plowed, and Clare returned to school. Most of the prisoners in the camp were moved north to the logging camps, but Peter and his friends remained to cut wood for Clare's father.

He and Clare didn't see much of each other, but whenever her father delivered potatoes to the camp, Clare went along so she and Peter could visit. They talked about Christmas now, and discovered they had some things in common in their celebrating. The angel at the top of the tree, the very old, fragile spun-glass ornaments, secret Santas, straws in the manger for good deeds done, caroling, and special Christmas treats.

Peter's favorite, he told her, was his mother's stollen, their Christmas morning coffeecake. He told her all the things that went into it, things she had never heard of, like citron, and how delicious it was. His father sliced the stollen at breakfast on Christmas morning, with the youngest child getting the heel, and the next youngest the first slice, and so on. "And we spread it with fresh, sweet butter. That is what I shall miss the most," Peter said, with a small sigh.

So Clare knew now what she would make him for Christmas. Her mother thought it a lovely idea but did she have a recipe? She looked in her Swedish cookbook, and yes, there was one! "And it must have cardamom seed in it, whether the recipe says so or not. Christmas bread is nothing without cardamom," she said firmly. "And of course, mashed potato. . . ."

They disagreed about the nuts. Clare's mother wanted to use the black walnuts they had stored in the cellar. "No," said Clare, who detested black walnuts. "They always taste moldy and dark. No, I'll go to Bouchard's Market and get almonds. That's what Peter's mother uses. And some candied cherries. And golden raisins, and an orange and a lemon. I don't know what citron is, but I don't think we need it." Clare was dancing with the pleasure of the whole thing. And she would buy everything with her own money.

On Christmas Eve morning, they cleared off the kitchen table and set to work. After Clare shelled the almonds, her mother boiled them a few moments, then plunged them into cold water and slipped them from their papery skins. Then she carefully sliced them into slivers.

While her mother made the dough, Clare crushed 10 cardamom seeds between sheets of wax paper with a rolling pin, releasing a warm, spicy smell unlike anything she had ever known. Then she grated the rinds from the lemon and the orange and added everything to the dough.

They set it to rise on a shelf above the stove, covering it with a damp towel. After it had risen to a round mountain, her mother punched it down and they added the raisins and cherries and almonds and let it rise again. Then Clare shaped it into an oval and folded it over, like a turnover. Her mother spread melted butter over the top, let it rise yet again, and then they put it into the oven with a prayer that their concoction would come out a stollen.

As it baked, an incredible, perfumey aroma filled the kitchen and eased out into the living room and upstairs and beyond the house. It brought Clare's father in from the barn. Clare's mother said, "I think we're going to have to make another one for us."

When it was done, the crust golden brown with bits of raisins and cherries peeking through to promise hidden delights, Clare's mother covered it with a glaze made from sugar and lemon juice. It was glorious.

That evening, Clare and her parents set off in the sleigh for the camp. They used the sleigh only on special occasions, like Christmas Eve, and winter ice-skating parties, and weddings. Clare and her mother were tucked in under wool quilts, the gifts for the prisoners on their laps. Clare's mother and aunts and grandmother had knitted wool caps and scarves for each of them, using odd bits of leftover yarn, so that no two were alike.

And they had made twelve stockings, cut from an old horse blanket and decorated with felt stars and bells and snowmen. Each contained an orange, an apple, hard candies in the shape of raspberries, green gummy spearmint Christmas trees, a gingerbread man with red hots for eyes, and a pen. Clare kept her gift for Peter in her lap, her hand protecting the red tissue wrapping, too fragile to keep in the good fragrance.

The snow had begun to fall lightly as the men came out from their barracks to greet their Christmas guests. Clare's father shook each of their hands and wished them a Merry Christmas and hoped that next year they would be home with their loved ones. Then Clare's mother wished them a Merry Christmas too and gave each man a stocking. The men seemed dazed. They stood awkwardly, the stockings clutched in their hands or folded to their chests.

Clare could wait no longer, and, bursting with pride, gave Peter the stollen. He opened the red tissue and broke out into delighted laughter. "I can't believe it. How did you ever do it? Clare, you are a very special person!"

"Take a bite right now, please, you must taste it!" begged Clare.

"If you don't mind, Clare, I would like to wait until after midnight, when it is truly Christmas, and we will all share it. But, wait, please. . . ."

He ran into the barracks and came out with his hands cupped around something. "I'm sorry I have no wrapping," he said and opened his hands. A small, plump wooden bird sat cheerily within, not minding at all the snow falling on it. "I carved it from a cherrywood burl . . . it was just the right shape. I could see the bird in it before I began to carve. It reminds me of you," said Peter.

Clare could think of nothing to say that would show how pleased she was. "Thank you, Peter. I shall keep it forever," she said at last, knowing she must be polite. She was afraid she would cry, and then she would feel foolish.

The prisoners began to whisper with each other, softly at first, then quickly, with confidence. Peter, their spokesman, bowed and addressed their guests.

"We would like to give you a gift, also, to thank you," he said. "It is very little, but we give it with all our hearts. *Gesegnete Weinachten!* Blessed Christmas!"

The prisoners began to sing in tones so clear, so true, it was as if their mingling of sweetness and rich depth was of one voice. The verses of *Stille Nacht, Heilege Nacht* pierced that still and holy night in

northern Maine, the voices rising into the crisp air, up and into the black, unending forests of pine, and the snow glistened with the tears on the cheeks of the men yearning for their families and the listeners yearning for their son and brother.

To Clare, no Christmas card scene would ever equal the beauty of this one of the German prisoners bundled up in their oversize overcoats, with their Christmas stockings held to their bosoms, singing to their enemies, exchanging gifts of love in a Christmas that would never happen again.

❋ ❋ ❋

In January, Peter and his friends joined the other prisoners in the logging camp up north. Within the year, the war was over and the men returned to Germany. Patrick and many of the young men of the town returned to Maine and their lives on the potato farms.

Clare did keep the bird for as long as she lived. It sat on the fireplace mantel in an honored position next to photographs of her parents, her wedding day, her children and grandchildren. She never tired of telling the newest grandchild the story of the bird and the young man who carved it and who picked potato bugs for her.

Peter became a minister, and each year he told the story of his Christmas Eve as a prisoner of war, until his congregation knew it by heart. He married and raised a family, and every Christmas, his wife, who was an excellent cook, baked a stollen. Peter, kindhearted husband that he was, praised it, but in his heart, he knew it could not compare with Clare's. No stollen ever could. Something was always missing, but he could not put his finger on it. It never occurred to him that its mystery ingredient was potato.

✳

UGNSPANNKAKA
SWEDISH PANCAKE

¼ cup butter or margarine
3 eggs, beaten
½ cup flour
¾ cup milk

Melt butter or margarine in pan (cast-iron skillet) in oven. Swish to coat bottom and sides of pan. Add flour to beaten eggs and gradually add the milk. Pour batter into pan and blend with melted butter. Bake in 400 degree oven for about 20 minutes. Serve with fresh berries and cream or fresh berry sauce.

—from *Favorite Swedish and American Recipes,* compiled by Members and Friends of Gustaf Adolph Lutheran Church, New Sweden, Maine.

✳

CLARE'S STOLLEN

1 pkg. dry yeast
½ cup lukewarm water
1 cup milk
½ cup butter
½ cup sugar
½ tsp. salt
1 cup mashed potatoes
2 eggs, beaten
grated rind of 1 orange and 1 lemon
10 cardamom seeds, crushed
4 to 5 cups flour
1 cup slivered almonds
1 cup candied cherries
1 cup golden raisins

Stir yeast into warm water and let sit about 5 minutes. Scald milk, add butter, sugar, salt, and potatoes in large bowl. Stir in eggs, rinds, cardamom.

Add yeast and stir in enough flour to make a stiff dough. Knead on floured table until smooth and elastic. Place in greased bowl and cover tightly. Let rise for an hour, or until doubled, and add nuts and fruit. Let rise again.

Shape into long oval, fold over at the center, brush with melted butter. Let rise, then bake at 400 degrees 15 to 20 minutes. Glaze if desired.

ISBN 0-89272-392-0

Color separations by Roxmont Graphics
Printed in Hong Kong through
Regent Publishing Services Ltd

4   2   5   3

Down East Books / Camden, Maine

Library of Congress Cataloging-in-Publication Data

Pochocki, Ethel, 1925–
     A penny for a hundred / by Ethel Pochocki ; pictures by Mary Beth
Owens.
          p.   cm.
     Summary: In 1944, in northern Maine, a nine-year-old girl
befriends a German prisoner of war who works with her in her
father's potato fields. Includes recipes for Swedish pancakes and
stollen.
     ISBN 0-89272-392-0
     [1. Prisoners of war--Fiction. 2. Farm life--Maine--Fiction.
3. Friendship--Fiction.] I. Owens, Mary Beth, ill. II. Title.
PZ7.P7495Pe   1996
[Fic]--dc20   96-30287
                                                                         CIP
                                                                          AC